When Bear Came Down from the Sky

TOLD BY **Tree de Gerez** • ILLUSTRATED BY **Lisa Desimini**

VIKING

VIKING
Published by the Penguin Group
Penguin Books USA Inc., 375 Hudson Street, New York, New York 10014, U.S.A.
Penguin Books Ltd, 27 Wrights Lane, London W8 5TZ, England
Penguin Books Australia Ltd, Ringwood, Victoria, Australia
Penguin Books Canada Ltd, 10 Alcorn Avenue, Toronto, Ontario, Canada M4V 3B2
Penguin Books (N.Z.) Ltd, 182-190 Wairau Road, Auckland 10, New Zealand

Penguin Books Ltd, Registered Offices: Harmondsworth, Middlesex, England

First published in 1994 by Viking, a division of Penguin Books USA Inc.

1   3   5   7   9   10   8   6   4   2

Text copyright © Toni de Gerez, 1994
Illustrations copyright © Lisa Desimini, 1994
All rights reserved

Library of Congress Catalog Card Number: 94-60646
ISBN 0-670-85171-X

Printed in China
Set in Cloister

In the days when stones were turnips
and kept growing
and growing
and growing;
in the days when the sky was so low
it had to be propped up
with an old soup spoon . . .

That was when stories began,
and that was when Bear lived
in the city in the sky.

So now then,
we are in the story
and the story begins.

As I told you,
  Bear lived in the sky
    with his family of stars—
Otava and his seven brothers.
Look, there they are!
                Look hard.
Bear was happy
      living in his big house
         in the sky.

Most of all, he liked looking out of the big sky window with pale blue cloud curtains.

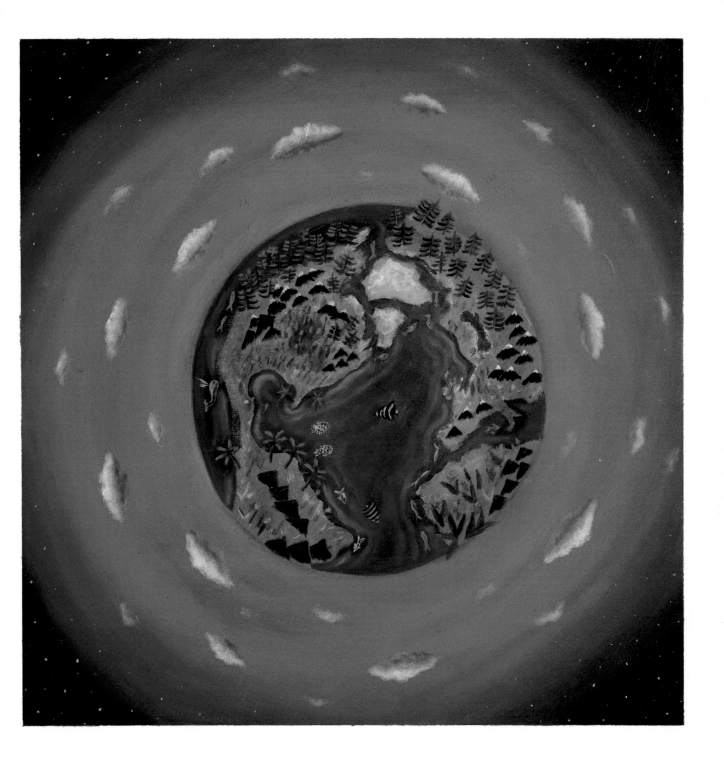

Bear liked asking questions. He asked, "Is that earth down there? Who is in charge? Who is Earth Maker? Do mountains talk to each other? What are trees? What is grass?"

Bear asked many questions.
Sky Father shook his head.
"Those are very big questions,
                    Bear my son."

Bear said proudly,
"I know many things
        about the sun and the moon."
Again he asked,
"What is earth?
            Is it a good place?

"I have heard about people.
            Do they sing?
                        Do they dance?
Do they have fur coats like mine?
Do they make bear tracks
                and bear noises?"

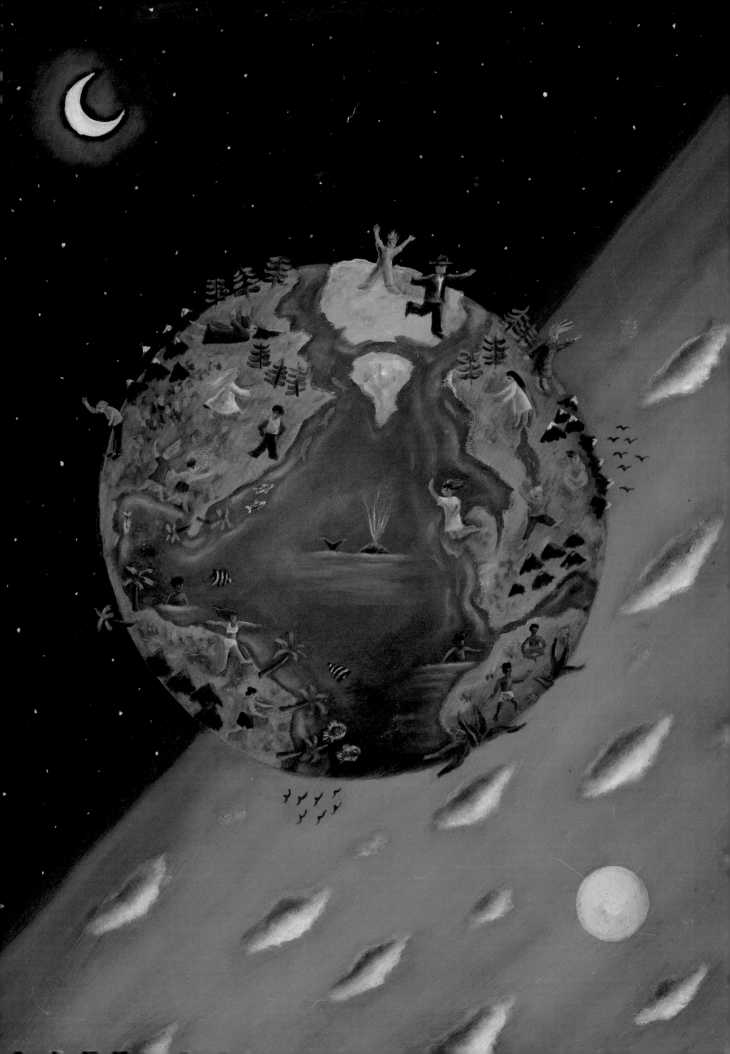

Bear was always asking
            up-and-down questions.
One day Sky Father said crossly,
"Why don't you go down
            and find out for yourself?
But I must tell you my son,
   you will not be able
      to come back to your sky home,
         so think about that."

Bear made up his mind.
"I will make a fine ladder
            and climb down."
But his ladder was not long enough
            to reach from the sky down,
                  down to the earth.

And so a basket was made just big enough for Bear to sit in:
a basket of golden coins with a long, long, silver, shining chain.

Bear said good-bye and sat down in his basket. Sky Father
shouted, "Be careful of man, eat the good berries, and don't
forget, sleep half the winter."

Bear sat in his gold and silver basket, and down, down he floated. Bear rode over cloud mountains and over cloud meadows and through pale sky air . . .

Until—until his basket caught on something. It was the very top of a very tall pine tree. Think of that!

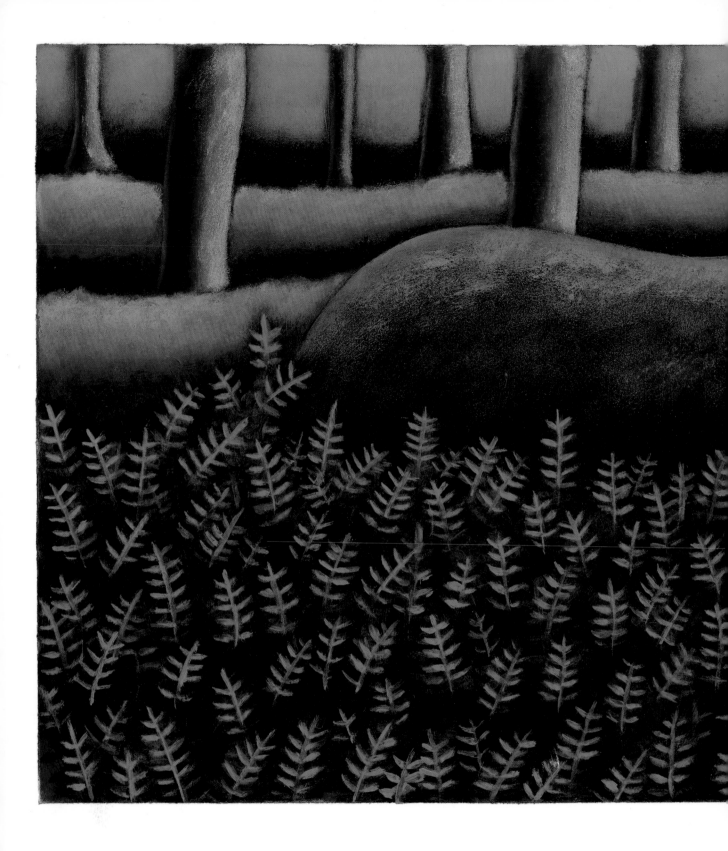

Bear fell out. Bear slid down over dark pine needles and tumbled onto the ground. Bear was on earth. He was in a soft bed of ferns and mosses.

Bear sniffed and sniffed with his stub stubby nose. Is this what earth smells like? he wondered. Green grass, green leaves. Green moss tickled his toes.

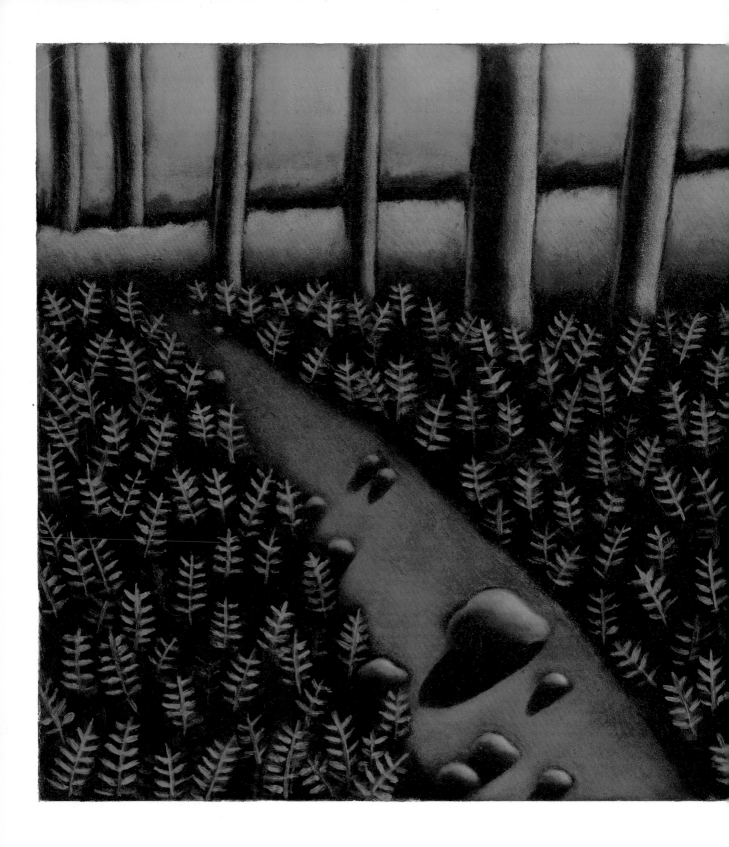

Bear laughed and started walking. "I'll find my own little path." And Bear went on his way and went on his way.

He stumbled on a rock. Rock said crossly, "Look where you're going."

Bear walked on and on. He was beginning to feel a lonely
feeling, a lost and lonely feeling in the big wood, when a soft
voice said . . .

"Don't be lonely, Bear. We have come to welcome you. We
have come to comfort you.

"I am Tellervo, Lady of the Green Dress. Tapio is my hus-
band, Keeper of the Big Word. We welcome you to our forest.
And in our forest you will be called Honey Paw.

"Come! Give me your paw. We will dance a round dance because the earth is round."

They danced together round and round.

Now Bear was hungry.
"I'll look for some brambles."
To keep himself brave
     he sang a little song.
It went like this:
  Bramble bramble bramble berries,
  I'll eat my belly full. . . .

And that's exactly what he did.
     All kinds of berries.
How good they tasted!
     And he ate his belly full.

Bear rested awhile on an old stump. "My name is Honey Paw," he told Stump. But Stump did not feel like talking. "Well, I'll go on my way," said Bear, and Bear went on his way.

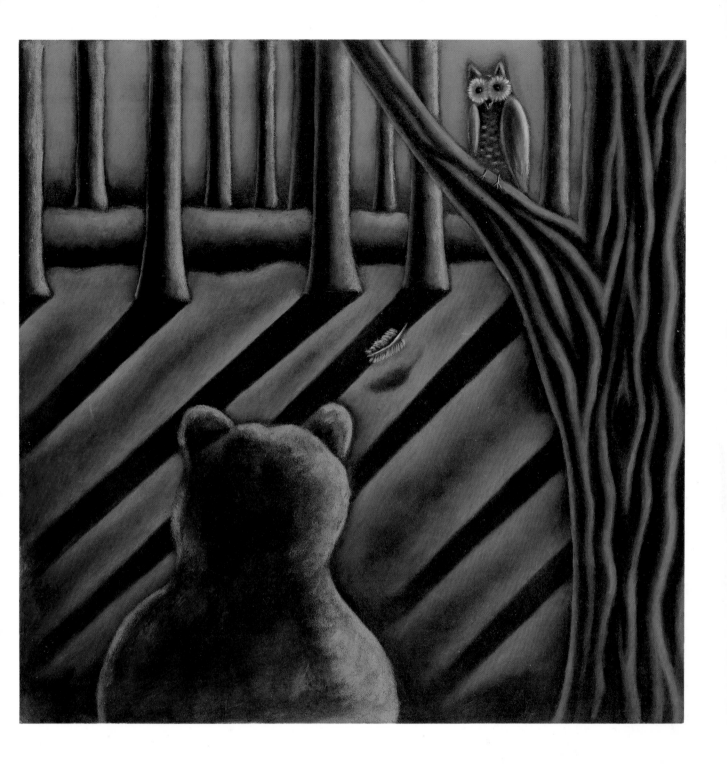

He saw an owl in a tree branch. He waved to Owl. A feather
drifted down. And then something happened. Bear did not
look where he was going.

He stepped right into the middle of an anthill. Now there was
trouble.

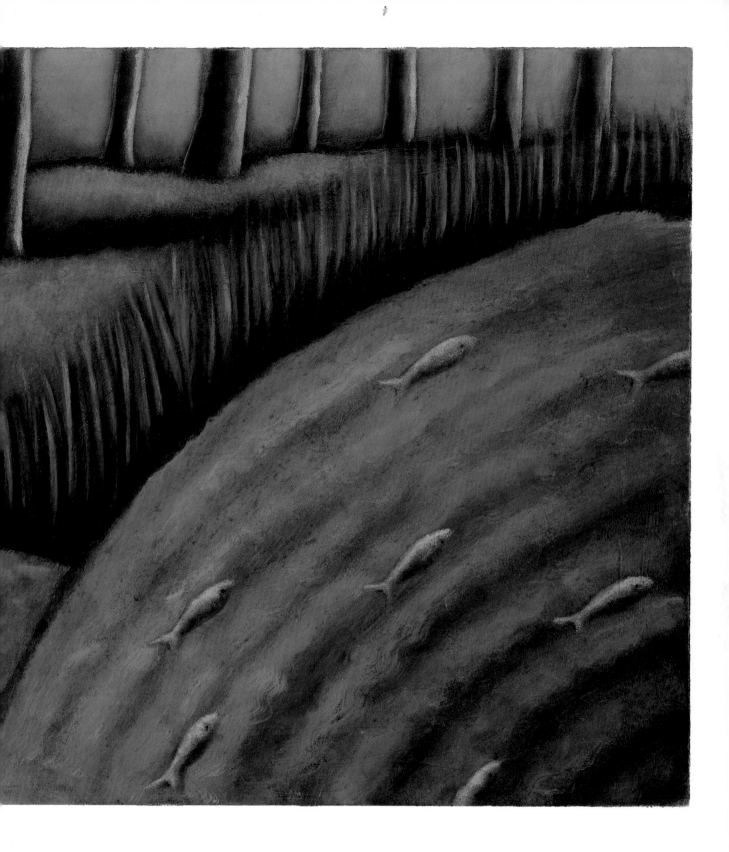

Ants were crawling all over poor Bear. So he began to run,
and he ran faster and faster right to a little old pond.

He jumped—*splash*—into the water, and that was the end of the ants. Bear climbed out of the water and shook himself. "I hope I don't catch cold," Bear said.

Time went by as time does. Bear learned how to live in the forest. He learned all kinds of things: How to eat golden bees. How to lap up brown ants. And how to catch a leaping silver trout.

Then one day the leaves began to change their summer green
to red and yellow. Bear admired them. "How beautiful you
are," he said.

But the leaves began to fall. Birds began to fly away. Bear
cried, "Please stay with me. Please stay."

Then one day snow began to fall.
"Snowflake, Snowflake,"
Bear cried,
    "what shall I do
        in this white forest alone?"

Bear remembered his Sky Father's words.
"When winter comes,
  winter cold and ice and snow,
    you must make yourself a little den.
Your bed will be soft with moss
        and pine needles and leaves.
This will be your own sleeping place.
    But don't forget,
      turn over half the winter through."

So that's what Bear did. There he is, hidden in his home.
Look! There is his blowhole.

Bear is safe and warm underneath in his bed. He is sleeping
and sucking his paw. He is humming a little bear song. Listen!

Nun nun nun nu

Ku lullu luu luu